Windy City Whirl

Penn Mullin

High Noon Books
Novato, California

Cover Design and Interior Illustrations: Damon Rarey

International Standard Book Number: 0-87879-961-3

9 8 7 6 5 4 3 2 1 0
4 3 2 1 0 9 8 7 6 5

You'll enjoy all the High Noon Books. Write for
a free full list of titles.

Contents

All aboard! Juan; Mike, their van driver; Justin; Miss Lake, their teacher; Amy; and Lisa smile for the camera before taking off on their trip.

When Miss Lake's seventh grade class entered the President's *See America the Beautiful* contest, they didn't think they had a chance to win. It was fun thinking they might, so everyone wrote and sent in a short essay on "What Do You Like Best About Being an American?"

They could hardly believe it when the letter came. It said: "The essays sent in by four members of your class were outstanding. These students have won a three-week trip across the United States with their teacher. All expenses will be paid."

The class clapped when Miss Lake finished reading the letter and Lisa, Amy, Justin, and Juan went home to pack their bags.

CHAPTER 1

The Top of the World

"Are you ready to go to the top of the world?" Miss Lake asked the kids.

"Let's do it!" Justin said.

"Push the button," said Miss Lake.

Justin pushed the elevator button for Chicago's Sears Tower building.

"Whoa! I think I left my stomach on the ground!" Amy said. "This thing really moves!"

"We are going 1800 feet per minute," Miss Lake told the kids.

"This is the tallest building in the world, right?" Lisa asked.

"Yes, it is 1,107 feet high," Miss Lake said. "One hundred and eighteen stories."

"I can feel it slowing down!" Lisa said.

The speeding elevator came to a stop.

"My ears are popping," Justin said.

The door opened. The kids and their teacher stepped out. They were on the Skydeck. It covered the whole floor. There was glass all the way around the sides.

"Wow! You can see forever from up here," Amy said.

"You can look into four states," Miss Lake said. "You can see Illinois, Indiana, Wisconsin, and Michigan from here."

Chicago's Skyline Today

"Listen to that wind roar!" Juan said.

"I think I feel it swaying." Amy suddenly looked scared.

"This was built to take high winds. It is supposed to sway a little," Miss Lake said.

"Lake Michigan looks like an ocean out there," Juan said. "I can see tons of sailboats. And the beaches go for miles."

"Chicago is lucky to be right on the lake," said Miss Lake. "The breezes cool the city off all summer. People can swim and sail without ever leaving town."

"Can we swim in the lake while we're here?" Justin asked their teacher.

"Sounds like a good idea," she said. "We just have to find the time."

"What is that river coming in from the lake?" Juan asked. He pointed straight down.

"The Chicago River. Cargo boats can come in there and then down to the Mississippi River. So you can see why Chicago is a good port city," Miss Lake told the kids.

"Look down at the river bank beside that bridge," Miss Lake said. "That's where Chicago first started. Can you believe there was once a fort there with nothing around it?"

"And it's total city now," Justin said.

"But in 1803 Fort Dearborn stood there. It was built by the first settlers here," said Miss

Lake. "This was when they were trying to decide who had the right to the land. You see, members of the Native American Potawatomi tribe were the first people to live here. They were the ones who gave Chicago its name."

"What did they call it?" Juan asked.

"*Che-cau-gua*, which meant wild onion or skunkcabbage," Miss Lake said.

"What did those words have to do with Chicago?" Amy asked.

"Well, this was then a very swampy, smelly place," Miss Lake told her.

"How long had the Native Americans been here?" Juan asked.

"Hundreds of years," Miss Lake said.

"They had shared the land with French explorers and fur trappers. Then came a Black Frenchman named Jean Baptiste Point du Sable. He built the first trading post here in 1781. Furs were traded for supplies and money. And Chicago has been growing ever since!"

"How many people live here now?" Justin asked.

"More than three million, with another four million in the suburbs," Miss Lake said.

"Didn't the city burn down once?" Lisa asked. "I heard a story about a cow kicking over a lantern and starting a fire."

"Yes, Mrs. O'Leary's cow," Miss Lake laughed. "People said the Great Fire of 1871 began in her barn."

"Is that true?" Lisa asked.

"No one knows for sure," said Miss Lake. "But I will tell you more about the fire tonight. And we will be in the perfect place."

"Where?" asked all the kids at once.

"The O'Leary Inn," chuckled Miss Lake. "They say it stands right where the old barn once did."

"This sounds spooky already!" Amy said.

"Wait till tonight!" Miss Lake smiled.

"I wonder if the O'Leary Inn has postcards," Amy said. "It's my turn to write one to send back to school."

The O'Leary Inn as It Might Have Been

CHAPTER 2

The O'Leary Inn

"This is it," said Mike, the van driver. "The O'Leary Inn! Once home of the famous cow that started the Chicago Fire."

They all looked out the windows at the inn. It was an old gray stone building standing on a narrow street. White flowers filled the windowboxes on all four floors.

"This looks really old. And kind of creepy!" Amy said.

"I think it looks great!" said Justin.

"OK, everybody. Let's unload," Mike said.

Everyone picked up a suitcase and followed Miss Lake and Mike into the inn.

"Good afternoon! We've been expecting you." The voice came from somewhere low inside the front door. They all looked down at a tiny white-haired lady in a wheelchair. "I'm Ella O'Leary and I own the O'Leary Inn."

Miss Lake told Ella everyone's name. "We're so glad you had room for us," she added. "This looks like a wonderful place."

"I think it's very special," Ella said. "It's been in my family a long long time. Ever since the fire. So there's lots of history here."

"Then this really was where the old barn

stood? The place where the fire started?" Lisa asked.

"This was the O'Leary barn. People still don't agree if the fire started here. But my family has always thought it did," Ella said.

Just then a tall thin man came in the door.

"Oh, this is Frank Moss, my helper here at the inn," Ella said, looking up at the man.

"Welcome to O'Leary's," Frank said. "We hope you'll enjoy your stay." His smile faded quickly. Then he stood there studying the group.

"Come on, I'll show you your rooms," Ella said. She wheeled herself towards the elevator.

Everyone picked up a suitcase and

followed her down the hall. The walls were covered with old photographs. The kids kept stopping to get a closer look.

"I'll show you all the pictures while you're here," Ella said.

Mike held open the elevator door for Ella.

"We'll have to take turns going up. This is really an old elevator. There's not much room inside," Ella said. "But I can take three of you with me now."

Amy, Lisa, and Miss Lake got into the elevator with Ella. Mike and the boys waited in the hall.

The elevator creaked slowly upward. "You're on the top floor," Ella said. "You'll have a nice view of the little street out front."

They got to the top floor. Ella pushed open the elevator door with her foot.

"I've gotten very good at that trick," Ella said. "There's not much I can't do here at the inn."

"You do really well," Miss Lake said. "I think you're amazing."

"I used to do it all myself. But then when I went lame, I had to get some help." Ella looked down at her legs. "I had to hire a helper. Frank." Her voice sounded troubled when she said his name.

Suddenly they heard a loud meow. A large fluffy grey cat came purring towards them.

"Oh, there you are, Felix. Where have you been hiding?" Ella smiled as the cat jumped up into her lap. "He doesn't like Frank at all. So he always stays upstairs."

"How long has Frank been here?" Miss Lake asked.

"About six months now. And things have started to change. Little things. But you don't want to hear this. You're on vacation. And you've got some great children with you!" Ella smiled up at Lisa and Amy. They walked beside her wheelchair and petted Felix.

Ella stopped in front of the last room on the hall. "Here you are. One of my very favorite rooms. Lots of light. Go on in. Take a look out the windows."

"It's beautiful!" Amy said when she walked into the room. "I love the tiny flowers on the wallpaper."

Lisa looked out the window. "This is such a neat little street we're on. Like our own secret hideaway in Chicago."

"I love the quietness," Miss Lake said. "What a wonderful inn you have here, Ella."

Ella smiled happily. "I'm glad you like it. That's what I love to hear! Now I had better go back down and get the others. Be sure to tell me if you need anything." She waved and started wheeling her chair back to the elevator. Felix rode happily on her lap.

"I'll open the door for you," Lisa said. She ran ahead of Ella down the hall.

"Don't worry. The door will open by itself, dear. I have a secret button on the floor," Ella told Lisa. "I just roll over it, and bingo—the door opens!"

"Hey, that's great," Lisa said as she watched. But just before the door closed, Felix jumped down from Ella's lap.

"See you later!" Ella waved to Lisa. Lisa picked up Felix and went back to the room. Amy and Miss Lake were talking.

"Isn't Ella a neat lady?" Lisa said.

"She sure is," Miss Lake agreed. "And a brave one. I am sure it must be hard to run an inn from a wheelchair."

"That Frank seems to be a problem," Amy whispered. "Too bad she had to hire him."

"Yes, Ella is not very happy. She must have some good reasons. Something bothered me about Frank, too, right away," said Miss Lake. "I think there's something strange going on in this old inn."

CHAPTER 3

Ghost Stories

"Hey, this is a great old place, isn't it?" Justin said. Miss Lake, Mike, and all the kids were standing by the front door of the inn.

"It sure is, Justin. Glad you like it. Did you get a chance to look at any of the old pictures yet?" Miss Lake asked.

"Not yet. Ella promised she would tell us about them tonight," he said. "Her great great grandmother took a lot of the pictures."

"Great. We'll all listen. It will be a

wonderful history lesson on Chicago!" Mike said.

"It's time we started for the baseball game," Juan said.

"You're right," Miss Lake answered. "It will be fun to see the Cubs play. I sure hope they win today! They have a brand new stadium, you know."

"Well, the van is ready," Mike said.

"Miss Lake, is it OK if I don't go with you? I'm feeling really tired," Amy said.

"Sure, Amy. Why don't you take a nap? We will tell you all about it when we get back," Miss Lake said.

Just then Ella came around the corner in

her wheelchair. She was smiling.

"Looks like you're off to the ball game. It's a great day for it," she said. "I wish I were going with you."

"Amy is going to stay here and take a nap, Ella," Miss Lake said. "Will you be here while we are gone?"

"Oh, yes. I'm not going anywhere. I'll be here if she wants anything."

"OK, we will be back in a couple of hours. Does everyone have some pocket money for hot dogs?" Miss Lake asked.

"Yes, let's go!" they answered together. "Bye, Amy, wish you were coming."

Amy and Ella watched the group get on

the van. Then they went back inside the inn.

"Felix is up on my bed," Amy told Ella. "He looks like he's there for the rest of the day."

"He'll probably stick close to you. I guess he knows a cat lover when he sees one!" Ella laughed.

Just then Frank stepped out of the elevator. He was not smiling. He came towards Amy and Ella.

"Three more people called today. They aren't coming," he told Ella. "And two yesterday. Things aren't looking good," he said. "I guess people have heard about our ghosts."

"Ghosts!" Amy said.

Ella gave Frank a puzzled look. Then she said, "Oh, it's a long story." Her voice sounded very tired. "People have said they saw ghosts in the halls. They told other people. Then people stopped coming. Even some of our oldest customers," Ella said sadly. "We just can't afford to have people cancel their rooms."

"I don't know how long we can go on this way," Frank said. He looked through the pages of a notebook on the desk. "Next month is almost empty. Hardly any rooms are filled."

"When did the ghost thing start?" Amy asked.

Frank gave her a sharp look.

"Oh, I guess it was about five or six months ago," Ella said. "There started to be some strange noises down in the cellar. And then there were the stories about ghosts."

"And screams in the night," Frank added.

"Did you ever call the police? Did you check out the cellar?" Amy asked.

"We thought it would not look good for the inn if we called the police," Frank said. "But we did check out the cellar. Found nothing."

"But the screams still kept up. And the guests still saw ghosts," Ella said sadly.

The cellar is a pretty awful place," Frank said. "Just perfect for ghosts. We need to go in there and get rid of all the old junk. You could turn it into a nice game room or something. It's a shame to leave that old cellar the way it is."

"But the cellar is *history*!" Ella said. "That's where the old barn was. I'll take you all down there tonight, Amy. There's lots to see."

"Oh, that would be great!" Amy said happily.

"Just hope the ghosts aren't down there with you tonight." Frank smiled a strange smile.

Ella looked at Frank and then turned her wheelchair around. "I think I'll go work at my desk awhile," she said. "Amy, you take a good nap. We'll all get together after dinner."

"OK. I'll see you later." Amy watched Ella wheel her chair down the hall. Then she started towards the elevator. As she walked she could hear Frank humming softly to himself at the front desk. For some reason she shivered as she opened the elevator door.

CHAPTER 4

Felix

Amy didn't know how long she had been asleep. But suddenly she was awake. Felix had awakened her with a loud hiss and a snarl. He had been asleep beside her on the bed. But now he was standing up with his back arched. He was staring at the door.

"What is it, Felix? What's the matter?" Amy asked him. "Is someone out there?"

Amy was wide awake now. And suddenly scared. Had she remembered to lock her door?

She listened. There was no sound outside. But Felix kept his eyes on the door.

Amy held her breath. She knew there was someone, or something, outside her door. Her heart pounded. She wished Miss Lake and the kids were back. Maybe it was just Juan or Justin playing a trick on her. But Felix—why was he acting this way? He really didn't like what was out there. Then Amy remembered. Frank. Felix didn't like him at all. Was Frank out in the hall right now?

Suddenly Amy heard voices. They were loud. They were coming out of the elevator. The kids were back! Amy pulled open the door to her room. She *had* forgotten to lock it. Miss

Lake, Mike, and the kids were all coming down the hall.

"Hi! Boy, am I ever glad you're back!" Amy said.

"Why? Is something the matter, Amy?" asked Miss Lake. "You look as if you've seen a ghost! I was hoping you would be asleep."

"Was anyone in the hall when you got off the elevator?" Amy asked.

"No. It was empty. Why?" Miss Lake said.

"I think there was someone outside our room just now. Felix knew there was. You should have seen how he was looking at the door," Amy said. Her voice was suddenly shaking.

"But look at Felix now," Lisa said. "Back to sleep," she laughed. Felix had curled himself into a ball at the end of the bed.

"Was Frank downstairs when you came in?" Amy asked.

"No, we didn't see him," Lisa said. "Why?"

"Hmmmm. I was just wondering. Don't you remember how Ella said Felix doesn't like Frank? Maybe he was out in the hall," Amy said.

"Well, maybe. He could have been walking in the hall," Miss Lake said.

"I really think there's something not right going on," Amy said. "Wait till you hear what Ella told me."

CHAPTER 5

Into the Cellar

Dinner was over. They had all gone out for Chicago deepdish pizza. Now they were back at the front door of the inn.

"Wow, I can never go back to plain old pizza again," Justin said. "That Chicago style was totally the best. So thick."

"You sure ate enough," Lisa laughed.

"Well, that was a long ball game. I was hungry!" said Justin. "I'm *still* hungry!"

"Who's ready to see some old pictures of

the Great Fire?" Ella asked as she joined everyone at the door. "Then we'll go down to see what's left of the old barn."

"Great!" Miss Lake said. "You're wonderful to show us. Lead the way!"

Ella wheeled herself towards the first pictures in the hall. Everybody followed her. Frank was nowhere in sight.

"This first picture shows Chicago in 1870, right before the fire," Ella said. "You can see it was quite a big city even then. But look how many wooden buildings there were. Ella used a yardstick to point up at the pictures from her wheelchair.

The next picture showed flames climbing

1871—The Fire!

high above the city. Black smoke filled the sky. There was nothing but fire—everywhere. "This is a very special photograph. October 8, 1871, the day of the Great Fire. My great great grandmother took it from a rooftop. She nearly died trying to escape before that building burned."

"How much of the city burned up?" Juan asked.

"Most of the downtown and the homes on the North Side," Ella said. "Ninety thousand people were left homeless. And 300 lost their lives in the fire."

"How long did the fire last?" Amy asked.

"It burned for more than 24 hours," Ella

said. "The city was so dry. It had been a long hot summer with little rain. Here is a picture of people trying to get away from the fire. This was taken right near here. When the barn burned, the winds swept the fire quickly. It jumped the river and chased people northward."

"Is that Lake Michigan?" Justin asked.

"Yes. People were running into the water to escape the fire," Ella said. "It was a terrible 24 hours."

"What finally stopped the fire?" Mike asked.

"Rain and also gunpowder. They blew up buildings that were in the path of the flames. This stopped the fire at last," Ella said. "Now look at this last picture. Can you believe this was Chicago just two years after the fire?"

"Amazing!" said Miss Lake. "You would never know there had been a fire. The city rebuilt itself so fast!"

"Chicago is tough. No wonder they call it the City of the Big Shoulders. It wasn't going to let the fire slow it down." Ella smiled.

"What was left of the old barn after the fire?" Lisa asked.

"Not much," Ella said. "But you can still tell it was a barn. Let's go down and I'll show you. Are you ready to step back into history?"

CHAPTER 6

Caught!

Ella rode the elevator down to the cellar. Everyone else took the old winding stairs. Felix decided to leave the fourth floor and come with them, too.

"This is really something else!" Justin said as they went down the stairs.

"I think it's a little creepy," Lisa said. "Are there lights down here?"

Suddenly the lights went on. Ella was waiting for them. "Here it is. My great great grandmother's barn. Or what's left of it. Look, you can still see the cow stalls here. They were made out of stone, so they did not burn. And over here they kept the hay."

"So right here the cow might have kicked over the lantern," Juan said.

"That's right. You're standing in the middle of history," Ella laughed.

"I can see burned places on these wooden floor boards," Mike said.

"I knew you all would like this," Ella said. "It's really a special place. I hate to think of ever changing it. That's what Frank wants—to clean it all out. But I like all the old things down here." She pointed to the old tools hanging on the walls. "They all somehow lasted through the fire."

Suddenly the lights went out. No one said a word. It was total darkness.

"Ella, are you OK?" Miss Lake asked. "Maybe a fuse blew. Tell me where the lights turn on. I'll try them."

"At the bottom of the stairs." Ella's voice sounded shakey. "Be careful. Don't fall. I can't find the switch here."

Miss Lake found her way to the stairs and tried the switch. "Nothing," she said.

"I don't like this," Lisa said.

"I'll go upstairs and check the fuse box," Mike said. "Frank can help me."

"Thanks, Mike," Ella told him.

Mike started up the stairs.

"This place sure got creepy in a hurry," Juan said. "I'm ready for some lights."

"I'm with you," Justin said.

"The door's locked!" Mike called down.

"Oh, no!" Ella cried.

Suddenly there was an awful scream from somewhere deep in the cellar. It wasn't a woman's scream. It wasn't a man's. It wasn't human.

Then there was silence. "Stay where you are, everybody," Mike said calmly.

"It's come back," Ella said. "That scream again. Why is this happening? I used to play down here when I was a little girl. There was nothing to be afraid of then."

Then there was another sound. Something was being dragged along the floor. Something in a far corner of the cellar.

Then there was a horrible yowl. "Felix!" cried Ella. "Where are you?"

"Help! Get him off me! Help!" A strange voice yelled. But a voice they all knew.

Justin and Juan hurried towards it in the darkness.

Felix kept yowling and hissing.

Now the boys could see a shape in the darkness. A tall man's shape. He was clawing at something that was on his back.

"It's Frank!" Justin cried.

"Get this cat off me!" Frank yelled.

"Frank. I should have known," Ella said. "It was you all the time. You've been the ghost. You've been the one scaring the guests away." She wheeled herself towards him. "You wanted me to have to sell the inn so you could take it over. Come here, Felix. You can let go of him now. You've done your work."

"Let's go upstairs," Miss Lake said. "Frank, do you have the key to the door?"

Frank mumbled something and handed her a key. Mike led them towards the stairs.

"Come on, Ella. I'll take the elevator up with you and Felix," Amy said.

"Fine! Oh, am I glad to find out what was causing all the trouble here! It's all over. Now people will start coming to the inn again. I can keep it open," Ella said happily. "I'm so glad that you kids won a trip to Chicago. And you decided to stay here." She and Felix got into the elevator with Amy.

Miss Lake and the other kids climbed up the stairs. Mike and Frank had gone ahead.

"Well, we never knew what adventures the O'Leary Inn would have for us, did we?" Miss Lake laughed.

"The inn's really great," Justin said. "I'm glad Ella will get to keep it now. Frank will be gone. She can get another person to help her."

43

"Good old Felix. What a brave cat!" Lisa said.

"What do we get to do tomorrow, Miss Lake?" Justin asked.

"We have about ten things to choose from," their teacher said. "Chicago has so much to see. How about a ride on the El train? Then the Museum of Science and Industy. That's where you'll get to go inside a submarine. And then the swim I promised you."

"Wow!" Juan said. "History, skyscrapers, submarines, and fantastic pizza! Chicago has it all!"

"And don't forget ghosts!" Lisa laughed.